To James (Jamie)

Always remember,
you
=
are special!

♡,
Amy
xoxoxo

Amy Sharpe was born and raised in Eastern Canada. She moved to Calgary with her husband, Jim, following graduation from Mount Allison University. She currently lives in Calgary with Jim and her three sons. Following the birth of her children, she began writing children's stories.

WALLACROCOGRIZZLEPHANT

AMY SHARPE

AUSTIN MACAULEY PUBLISHERS™
LONDON • CAMBRIDGE • NEW YORK • SHARJAH

Ordering Information:
Quantity sales: special discounts are available on quantity purchases by corporations, associations, and others. For details, contact the publisher at the address below.

Publisher's Cataloging-in-Publication data
Sharpe, Amy
Wallacrocogrizzlephant

ISBN 9781643788951   (Paperback)
ISBN 9781643788968   (Hardback)
ISBN 9781645365532   (ePub e-book)

Library of Congress Control Number: 2019910938

www.austinmacauley.com/us

First Published (2020)
Austin Macauley Publishers LLC
40 Wall Street, 28th Floor
New York, NY 10005
USA
mail-usa@austinmacauley.com
+1 (646) 5125767

Dedication

To Andrew, Thomas, and David.

Once upon a time,
there was a wallaby named "Joey."
He didn't look the same,
his ears were really showy.

His teeth were very big
and his claws were very long.
Compared to other wallabies. . .
he was very strong.

It used to bother Joey
that he had big claws and ears.
But then one day these special features
earned him praise and cheers.

Truth be told,
Joey wasn't just a wallaby.
He was a wallacrocogrizzlephant,
according to his family tree.

If you look back to his grandpa,
on his father's side,
you'll find a wallaby, named Joe,
and Sarah, his croco-bride.

Sarah had a baby boy.
This very much pleased Joe.
He was the apple of their eye,
....Jack, the Wallacroco!

Around that time,
 a grizzly bear named Gus began to know
an elephant named Molly,
and a love began to grow.

They soon had Jill, the Grizzlephant,
she was a sweet surprise.
She slept all winter long
and could blow water to the skies.

Then Jack met Jill, and she became,
his one true love in life.
So on one warm day in June,
Jack asked Jill to be his wife.

When Jack and Jill had Joey,
they moved back with the wallabies,
to be surrounded by their families' love,
and lush green plants and trees.

Now, did you know that wallabies
jump and box and play?
Joey and his cousins
used to play these games all day.

At times, his cousins
wouldn't let him in the boxing match.
They'd say he was too strong for them
and that his claws would scratch.

He couldn't win the jumping games.
He really couldn't jump.
His ears were far too heavy
and he'd land with a loud thump.

His mom and dad would tell him
to smile and not feel sad.
They'd say his features made him special
and that made him feel glad .

Then one morning,
Joey and his mob went out to play.
The game was so much fun,
that it led them far away...

When lunchtime came,
the little wallabies began to cry.
They couldn't find their way back home,
and the sun was high up in the sky.

Soon, they would have to find their home,
to get a drink.
So Joey stopped, sat,
and used his elephant brain to think!

When all the other wallabies were
crying and upset,
Joey found the way back home
because...
Elephants never forget!!!

Joey led them all back to their home
and to the water.
And with not much time to spare
because the day was getting hotter.

Joey knew he saved the day,
and that made him feel proud.
The parents in the mob all cheered,
and cheered for him quite loud!

Joey loved the cheering.
But Joey also knew
that a pack of wild dogs nearby
could hear the cheering too.

Joey knew that these wild dogs
would not be a friendly bunch.
'Cause most wild dogs do enjoy...
some wallabies for lunch!

The dogs came charging towards the mob
with hunger, speed and haste.
Joey knew that they were coming
and not a moment did he waste!

He told the moms and dads
to hide their babies in the brush.
He told them not to make a sound.
He told them to HUSH, HUSH!

Then Joey hid behind a tree,
with his claws stretched out each side.
So when the dogs looked up his way,
they quickly broke their stride.

What they saw was a tall tree
with hands and claws just like a bear.
So they stopped, gasped and turned around,
and ran far, far from there!

The wallabies came out again
when they knew the coast was clear.
Joey saved the day again!!!
And they cheered a QUIET cheer!

That's when Joey knew
his special features saved the day.
And from that day on, Joey
felt a different sort of way.

His mom and dad were right.
He SHOULD smile and not feel sad.
His features made him special
and that DID make him feel glad!!!

This story is about
how great our differences can be.
Your features make you, you.
My features make me, me.

So if you're feeling different,
just smile from ear to ear.
Different features make us special,
and THAT deserves a cheer!!!